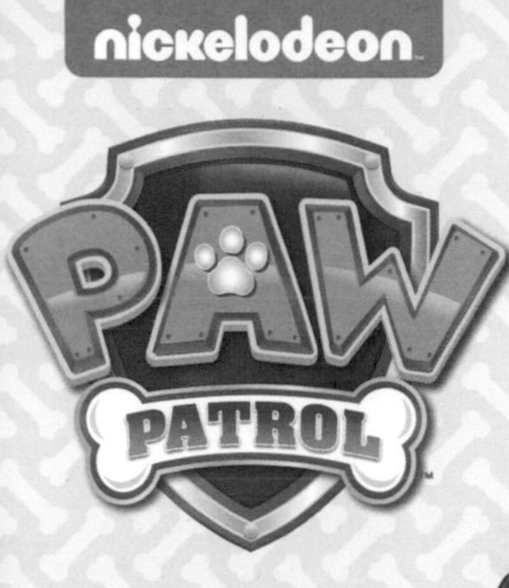

PAW PATROL ON THE ROLL!

A Random House PICTUREBACK® Book

Random House New York

 Published in the United States by Random House Children's Books, a division of Penguin Random House LLC, 1745 Broadway, New York, NY 10019, and in Canada by Random House of Canada, a division of Penguin Random House Ltd., Toronto. Pictureback, Random House, and the Random House colophon are registered trademarks of Penguin Random House LLC. PAW Patrol and all related titles, logos, and characters are trademarks of Spin Master, Ltd. Nickelodeon and all related titles and logos are trademarks of Viacom International Inc.
randomhousekids.com
ISBN 978-1-101-93867-6
MANUFACTURED IN CHINA
10 9 8 7 6 5 4

Lenticular cover effect and production: Red Bird Publishing Ltd., U.K.

When someone calls for help, the PAW Patrol race into action on their awesome vehicles.

"We can all ride in the PAW Patroller," Ryder says. "When we need to go on a rescue outside Adventure Bay, this big eighteen-wheeler can take the whole team—and our vehicles, too!

"For rescues closer to home, I hop on my speedy ATV," he explains. "At the touch of a button, it can change into a snowmobile or a Jet Ski!"

CHASE IS ON THE CASE!

"If you see these lights flashing and hear sirens blaring, you know I'm on the case in my police truck," says Chase. "The back has lots of room to store equipment, like orange safety cones, and the front has a winch for moving and towing big things."

Chase's truck can also turn into a spy mobile for super-spy missions!

Marshall's fire truck can turn into an ambulance when he needs to roll out on a medical rescue!

"You're in good paws when I roll to the rescue," barks Marshall. "My fire truck is prepared for every emergency. It has hoses and water pumps to put out fires, and ladders to reach high places."

"I'm always ready to fly," says Skye. "To take to the skies, I use my Pup Pack, with its pop-out wings! But if I'm traveling long distances, I need my helicopter."

Skye's high-flying helicopter has a claw to pick things up and a towline to carry special cargo.

Zuma uses his submarine’s claw to move really big objects.

"My hovercraft is a speedy machine on land and water," says Zuma. "It can sail over waves and launch life rings to those who need help.

"And with the press of a button, the craft becomes a submarine!"

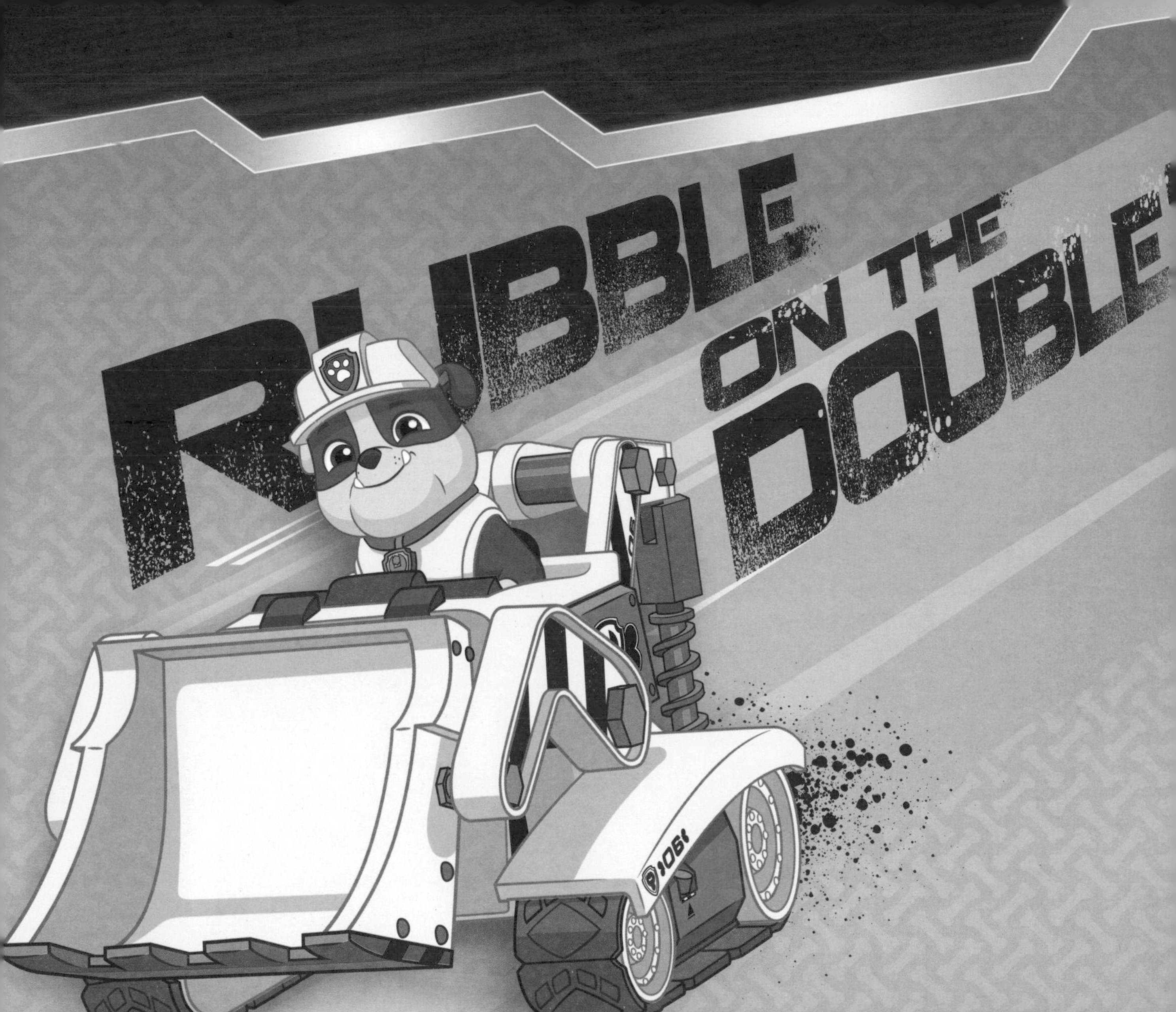

RUBBLE ON THE DOUBLE

"If the PAW Patrol needs some heavy lifting, I'm Rubble on the double with my bulldozer," barks Rubble.

Rubble's Digger has a giant shovel on the front to move dirt, and a powerful drill on the back.

With the bits and pieces he's saved in his truck, Rocky can fix everything from ladders to windmills.

"Don't lose it—reuse it!" says Rocky. "My recycling truck is perfect for that. The forklift on the front can pick up heavy loads. And the storage area in the back is where I keep my recycling."

“Winter rescues are no problem for me and my snowcat,” barks Everest. “These heavy-duty treads get me over icy hills, and the plow can clear any snowy road.”

If there’s a really big obstacle in the way, like a fallen tree, Everest’s plow has a claw that can pick it up and move it!

On land, in the air, or under the water, the PAW Patrol are always ready to lend a paw. Just yelp for help, and they'll be on the roll!